I SEE ...
THE BEACH

William Buning

ISBN: 979-8-396-36651-0

BUBA productions LLC
bubaproductionsllc@gmail.com

Author and Illustrator: William Buning
Editor in Chief: Lauren Buning
Associate Editor: Lillian Buning
Associate Editor: Liam Buning
Market Research Assistant: Oliver Buning

For my children Lillian, Liam, Oliver, and my amazing wife Lauren.

I am going to the beach today.

What animals will I see?

What do I see?

It's a Crab!

I wave to the Crab.

The Crab PINCHES back.

What do I see?

It's a Fish!

I wave to the Fish.

The Fish BUBBLES back.

What do I see?

It's an Octopus!

I wave to the Octopus.

The Octopus WAVES back.

What do I see?

It's a Sea Lion!

I wave to the
Sea Lion.

The Sea Lion ARH ARHS back.

What do I see?

It's a Seagull!

I wave to the Seagull.

The Seagull SQUAWKS back.

What do I see?

It's a Sea Turtle!

I wave to the
Sea Turtle.

The Sea Turtle
WINKS back.

What do I see?

It's a Dolphin!

I wave to the
Dolphin.

The Dolphin
EH EH EHS back.

It's time to leave the beach.

PINCH

BUBBLE

WAVE

I wave goodbye to all the animals.

ARH ARH

SQUAWK

WINK

EH EH EH

The End

PINCH

BUBBLE

WAVE

ARH ARH

SQUAWK

WINK

EH EH EH

Dear Reader,

I hope you enjoyed reading this book with your child. I was inspired to write a children's book by my own young children.

My 7-year-old loves to doodle, it is one of our favorite activities to do together. One day my 1 ½ year-old started to wave at the animals while my 4-year-old made the sounds. I used these doodles and sounds to create a handmade book. My youngest enjoyed it so much I thought why not make something a little more official and the *I See ...* series was born.

Making books interactive and fun is the best way to keep the attention of our youngest readers. That is why I have included features like asking questions, doing hand gestures, and making silly sounds part of this book.

Have fun and don't be scared to be silly!

Sincerely,
William Buning

Made in the USA
Coppell, TX
20 June 2023

18337594R10017